MT. PLEASANT LIBRARY
PLEASANTVILLE, NY

MOUSE AND MOLE
A PERFECT HALLOWEEN

Written and illustrated by
WONG HERBERT YEE

sandpiper

Green Light Readers
HOUGHTON MIFFLIN HARCOURT
BOSTON NEW YORK

For the boy in the skeleton costume

Copyright © 2011 by Wong Herbert Yee

First Green Light Readers edition 2012

All rights reserved. Published in the United States by Sandpiper, an imprint of Houghton Mifflin Harcourt Publishing Company. Originally published in hardcover in the United States by Houghton Mifflin Books for Children, an imprint of Houghton Mifflin Harcourt Publishing Company, 2011.

SANDPIPER and the SANDPIPER logo are trademarks Houghton Mifflin Harcourt Publishing Company.

Green Light Readers and its logo are trademarks of Houghton Mifflin Harcourt Publishing Company, registered in the United States of America and/or its jurisdictions.

For information about permission to reproduce selections from this book write to Permissions, Houghton Mifflin Harcourt Publishing Company, 215 Park Avenue South, New York, New York 10003.

www.hmhbooks.com

The text of this book was set in Adobe Caslon.
The illustrations were created in litho pencil and gouache.

The Library of Congress has cataloged the hardcover edition as follows:
Yee, Wong Herbert.
Mouse and Mole, a perfect Halloween/Wong Herbert Yee.
p.cm.
Summary: As Halloween approaches, Mouse helps her friend Mole get over his fear and enjoy the holiday.
[1. Best friends—Fiction. 2. Friendship—Fiction.
3. Halloween—Fiction. 4. Mice—Fiction. 5. Moles
(Animals)—Fiction.]
I. Title. II. Title: Perfect Halloween
PZ7.Y3655Mjp 2011
[E]—dc22   2010033432

ISBN: 978-0-547-55152-4
hardcover
ISBN: 978-0-547-85057-3
paperback

Manufactured in China
SCP 10 9 8 7 6 5 4 3

4500417300

CONTENTS

A SKELETON IN THE CLOSET

PERFECT PUMPKINS

THE CONTEST

FRAIDY-MOUSE,
SCAREDY-MOLE

A SKELETON IN THE CLOSET

Mouse looked at the calendar.

"Eek!" she squeaked.

"It's almost time for Halloween!

I had better get busy."

Snip, snip, snip!

Mouse cut out spiders.

Mouse cut out bats.

She taped them

to the window.

Next, Mouse took a skeleton from
the closet. She hung it up in the oak.
An autumn breeze rattled
the plastic bones:
Clickety-clack-clack!
"Spooky!" Mouse giggled.

Mouse twirled her tail.

"Something is missing . . ."

She spotted a flyer in the mailbox.

HALLOWEEN PUMPKIN
CARVING CONTEST!
Pick a pumpkin.
Carve the pumpkin.
Put the pumpkin in a box.
(So it will be a surprise!)
Judging on the night
before Halloween.

"Silly me," laughed Mouse.

"A *pumpkin* is
what I need!"

Mole tossed and turned in his sleep.
Something was following him . . .
Clickety-clack-clack! Mole peered over
his shoulder. "YIKES!" he hollered.
A skeleton was hot on his heels!

Down the path Mole sprinted.
He tripped and tumbled — *whump!*
Mole landed on the floor by
his bed. "Thank goodness
it was just a dream!"

Mole looked at the calendar.

Halloween was just

around the corner.

TAP-TAP-TAP.

A knock on the door

made Mole jump.

"Who is th-th-there?" he whispered.

"It's me, Mouse," said Mouse.

Mole opened the door a crack.

"There's a pumpkin contest in town!"

said Mouse. "Let's go get some

pumpkins to carve."

Mouse showed

Mole the flyer.

"A pumpkin contest is not
that scary," thought Mole.
He hurried to fetch the wagon.
Clickety-clack . . . SMACK!
Mole bumped into
Mouse's skeleton.

"YIKES!" he hollered.
Mole dashed back
into his hole.

PERFECT PUMPKINS

Mouse parked the wagon under an elm.

Whoosh! A gust of wind sent golden

leaves fluttering down.

"What a perfect autumn day," sighed Mouse.

"*Perfect* for picking pumpkins," said Mole.

"And a *perfect* pumpkin is what

I plan to pick!" announced Mouse.

Mouse skipped through the field, singing:

"Some are big, some are small!

Some are fat, some are tall!

Mercy me!" she squeaked.

"There are so many pumpkins

to choose from!"

Mouse twirled her tail.

Mouse covered her eyes.

"Eeny, meeny, miny mumpkin —

Which of you will be my pumpkin . . .?

You're it!" Mouse pointed.

Mole wandered about the pumpkin patch.

He gave each pumpkin a

TAP-TAP-TAP.

He turned them this

way and that.

Mole tugged on the stems.

Finally, he found one he liked.

"The perfect pumpkin!"

Mole proclaimed.

Mouse filled the wagon
with leaves.
Mole set the pumpkins on top.

Mouse's pumpkin was tall and thin.
Mole's was big and round.
Mouse looked at Mole's.
Mole looked at Mouse's.
"The perfect pumpkins!"
they laughed.

The contest was not until next week.

Mole, however, went to work at once.

To begin, he cut a hole around the stem.

Mole wiggled the top loose.

He scooped out the mush.

Next, Mole drew three triangles
for the eyes and nose.
He added a smile
with two perfectly
square teeth. Carefully,
Mole cut the shapes out.

"There!" he nodded. "My *perfect* pumpkin
is now the *perfect* jack-o'-lantern!"
Mole rubbed his snout.
"What if Mouse sees
my jack-o'-lantern?

What if Mouse wants to copy it?"
Mole took a box from the closet.
He put the pumpkin in the box and hid
it outside under a pile of leaves.

That night, Mole had a dream about the contest. In his dream, all the jack-o'-lanterns looked *exactly* like his!

Days later, Mole saw Mouse's pumpkin still sitting on the stoop. He knocked on her door: TAP-TAP-TAP. Slowly, it creaked open —

"**BOO!**" Out jumped a ghost.

"Yikes!" Mole hollered.

Mouse yanked the bed

sheet off. "Got you!"

She snickered.

Mouse tossed the bed sheet to Mole.

"You can draw the face on our ghost!"

"What about your pumpkin?"

Mole pointed.

"Tomorrow," Mouse said.

"There's still plenty of time."

Mole spread the white cloth on the floor.

He drew two eyes with a black marker.

Mole added a smile underneath.

"A friendly ghost is not that scary."

Mouse finished making a spider web
from string. She crept behind Mole
and flung it over him.
"EEP!" yelled Mole.
"Got you again!"
laughed Mouse.

Together, they strung the spider web across the doorway. "You left your broom on the porch," Mole noticed. "That's not my broom," cackled Mouse. "Perhaps a *witch* left it!"
Mole dashed back into his hole.

Mouse gazed out the window.

"Leaves are swirling, whirling–twirling,

yellow, red, and brown.

Leaves keep falling, falling-falling —

soon they'll all come down!"

Mouse glanced at the calendar.

"Goodness!" she cried.

"The contest is tonight!"

Quickly, Mouse lopped
the top off her pumpkin.
She scooped out the mush.
Next, Mouse cut two
circles for eyes.
One was a bit bigger
than the other.
"Whoops!" she giggled.
Mouse made a tiny slot for the nose.
Mouse carved a huge mouth
filled with pointy teeth.

She jammed the lid back on.

The stem broke off.

Mouse tapped her foot.

She ran outside and grabbed
a bunch of leaves.

Mouse stuffed them in the top.

"There!" she nodded.

"My *perfect* pumpkin is now
the *perfect* jack-o'-lantern!"

THE CONTEST

Mouse and Mole set their boxes
on the table.

"Good luck!" said Mole to Mouse.

"Good luck!" said Mouse to Mole.

Judge 1 lifted the first pumpkin out.

Judge 2 jotted down notes.

Judge 3 lit the candle inside.

Sometimes the audience gasped.

Sometimes they snickered.

Mole squirmed in his seat.

"Quit being such a wiggle worm!"

hissed Mouse.

Her pumpkin was next.

Judge 1 took it out of the box.

Judge 2 began scribbling like mad.

Judge 3 was laughing so hard, he blew out the candle.

One eye of Mouse's jack-o'-lantern was *twice* as big as the other. The nose was itty-bitty. The enormous mouth was packed with crooked teeth. Leaves sticking out the top gave the pumpkin a funny hairdo.

"That is just silly!"
chuckled Mole.
He crossed his fingers
behind his back.

Mole's pumpkin was the last one left.

Judge 1 shuddered while lifting it out!

Judge 2 dropped her notebook in fright!

Judge 3 fainted on the spot!

The crowd gasped in unison.

A baby began to cry.

Mole's jack-o'-lantern was sunken
and lumpy and smelly.
The once perfect eyes
were now squinty slits.
The smile had turned into a frown.
A dried worm dangled out the nose.
"Rats!" muttered Mole.
"Spooky!" Mouse giggled.
The judges huddled together.
"We have our winners!"
they declared.

Judge 1 slapped an orange ribbon on Mouse's pumpkin. "For the silliest jack-o'-lantern!"

Judge 2 flung a black ribbon at Mole's pumpkin. "For the sc-scariest j-jack-o'-lantern!"

Judge 3 nearly fainted again.

Mouse and Mole also won pillowcases for trick-or-treating. One was decorated like a skeleton, the other like a ghost. "Congratulations!" said Mouse to Mole. "Congratulations!" said Mole to Mouse. Everyone clapped and cheered.

Mouse and Mole put their pumpkins and pillowcases in the wagon.

Together, they headed down the

moonlit trail. *Bumpity-bump-bump!*

Mole peered nervously over his shoulder.

The wind sent leaves fluttering down.

One landed on Mole's head. "Eep!"

Mole pointed. "A giant spider!"

"Do not be silly,"

laughed Mouse.

She brushed the leaf off.

They continued along the path.

Mole froze once again. "Mouse . . .

is that a sk-skeleton touching me?"

Mouse lifted the twig off Mole's shoulder.

"Don't be such a *scaredy-Mole!*" she teased.

Whoosh! A huge gust of wind whipped

the pillowcases high in the air.

"Yikes!" Mole hollered.

"A G-G-GHOST!"

Down the path

he sprinted.

FRAIDY-MOUSE, SCAREDY-MOLE

That night, Mole tossed and turned in
his sleep. The skeleton was still after him.
A ghost and a witch had joined the chase.
Mole ran *smack* into a giant spider web!
He awoke all tangled in his blankets.

TAP-TAP-TAP.

A knock on the door
made Mole jump.

"Who is th-th-there?" he stammered.

"It's me, Mouse," said Mouse.

"Let's go pick costumes!"

Mole opened the door a crack.

"You g-g-go ahead, Mouse.

I am not sure about

tr-trick-or-treating."

Mouse tapped her foot.

Mouse twirled her tail.

Maybe scaring Mole was a mistake . . .

"I'll be right back," she called.

Mouse returned carrying a book.

"I'm going to read a story, Mole.

Perhaps it will make you less afraid."

"What *kind* of story?" Mole wondered.

"A Halloween story," said Mouse.

"But Halloween is sc-scary!" cried Mole.

"Scary, yes — but exciting too!"

Mouse began to read.

One Halloween a little Mouse
peers outside her little house.

Leaves whirl and twirl!
Mouse is afraid!
She locks the door
and pulls the shade.

"Is that *fraidy-Mouse* you?" Mole asked.

"Not really," said Mouse,

"but it could be."

Mole sat on the

edge of his seat.

Mouse continued reading.

One Halloween a tiny Mole
peeps out of his tiny hole.
He hears a squeaky-
CREAKY sound.

CREAK!
SQUEAK!

Zip! Mole ducks
back underground.

Mole interrupted Mouse once more.

"Is this *scaredy-Mole* me?" he asked.

"Not really," said Mouse,

"but it might be."

Mole rubbed his snout.

Mouse continued reading.

One Halloween a little Mouse
tiptoes from her little house.
Mouse sees a pair
of glowing eyes.
Eek! she squeaks.
What a surprise!

One Halloween a tiny Mole
creeps out from his tiny hole.
He hears an eerie-
SCARY sound.
Eep! Mole dives back
underground.

Mouse noticed Mole gripping the arms of his chair. "Are you okay?" she asked. "I am f-f-fine," said Mole. "Keep reading." Mouse went on with the story.

One Halloween a little Mouse ventures from her little house. It's so dark outside at night! Mouse runs home to fetch a light.

Down the path trots tiny Mole,
far, far from his tiny hole.
He sees a light!
Who could that be?
Mole darts behind the willow tree.

Down the path skips little Mouse,
far, far from her little house.
Mouse hears a crack!
What could that be?
She ducks behind the willow tree.

CRACK!

CRASH! Mole toppled right off his chair.

"Mole, are you okay?" squeaked Mouse.

"I will stop if it's too scary."

"NO!" begged Mole.
"It is scary, YES —
but *exciting* too!
Please continue."
Mouse giggled to herself.
"If you insist, Mole!"

Mouse shines the light into Mole's face.
They're sharing the same hiding place.

They both are dressed as vampire bats!
They both wear matching pumpkin hats!

Each has an empty pillowcase.
Mole takes off.
Mouse starts to chase.

Across the graveyard, in a ditch . . .
EEK! a vampire; EEP! a witch.

Along the fence, behind the post . . .
EEP! a skeleton; EEK! a ghost.

Mouse and Mole see a black cat.
What's so scary about that?

At every house lit down the street,
they stop and holler —

TRICK OR TREAT!

Though winds may howl,
and shadows wave . . .
Together, Mouse and Mole are brave!

Mouse shut the book.

"The End!" she announced.

Mole tapped his foot.

Mole rubbed his snout.

"Perhaps *I* could be like

tiny Mole?" he whispered.

Mouse smiled.

"Of course you can, Mole.

And *I* will be that *little Mouse!*"

Together, Mouse and Mole went to
the Halloween shop.

Mole picked out two vampire bat costumes.
Mouse found matching pumpkin hats.
Pillowcases they already had!

As soon as it got dark,
Mouse put on her costume.
TAP-TAP-TAP knocked
Mouse on Mole's door.
Slowly it creaked open . . .

"BOO!"
Out jumped
a ghost in
the doorway.

"EEK!" shrieked Mouse.
Mole yanked the
pillowcase off.
"Got you back!"
he chuckled.

Down the path Mole sprinted.

"Do not be such a *fraidy-Mouse!*"

Mole hollered.

Mouse could not help giggling.

Up the steps she scampered

after Mole.

Together, Mouse and Mole

had a *perfect* Halloween!

DISCARD MT. PLEASANT